EGMONT
We bring stories to life

First published in Great Britain 2011
by Egmont UK Limited
239 Kensington High Street, London W8 6SA

Editor: Catherine Such
Art Editor: Amanda Hartley
Designer: Nancy Dunkerley
Writer: Deborah Nash
Editorial Assistant: Hannah Greenfield
Group Art Editor: Jeanette Ryall
Group Editor: Keilly Swift

ISBN 978 1 4052 5694 0
1 3 5 7 9 10 8 6 4 2
Printed in Italy

Note to parents: adult supervision is recommended when sharp-pointed items such as scissors are in use.

This annual belongs to

Name:

Age:

Disney·PIXAR

TOY STORY

Disney·PIXAR

MONSTERS, INC.

Disney · PIXAR

FINDING NEMO

Disney · PIXAR

WALL·E

Disney PRESENTS A PIXAR FILM

THE INCREDIBLES

Toy Friend? Toy Foe?

Colour a star to show whether each Toy Story character is a friend or foe.

WOODY

A **cowboy sheriff** who cares about his toy friends and never gives up on them – not ever. He remains loyal to his owner, **Andy**, and climbs up walls and falls from trees for him.

FRIEND

FOE

JESSIE

FRIEND

FOE

Cowgirl and tomboy, **Jessie** is full of life. She's brave, adventurous and independent. She likes Spanish dancing with **Buzz**.

MR POTATO HEAD

A tough spud for others to crack, **Mr Potato Head** can take himself apart with ease and speed. He is not so happy when he becomes a sausage and a tortilla.

FRIEND

FOE

8

BIG BABY

Big Baby looks broken and mean and has a half-closed eye. He takes his orders from **Lotso** and keeps the toys prisoner at **Sunnyside**.

FRIEND

FOE

BUZZ LIGHTYEAR

He is a **space ranger** with a laser beam, pop-out wings and a karate action chop. All this to defeat enemies in outer space, but **Buzz** finds he has a mission much closer to home.

FRIEND

FOE

ALIENS

Three green multi-eyed squeak toys from **Pizza Planet**, the aliens save the toys from being roasted by operating **the claw**.

FRIEND

FOE

LOTSO

Head ted at **Sunnyside** Daycare Centre, **Lotso** is pink, smells of strawberries and looks like a friendly bear. But don't be fooled, he's not as cuddly as he appears.

FRIEND

FOE

Answers on page 68.

A New Nose

1 One evening at Sunnyside, when all of the children had gone home, Mr Potato Head sat up. "Boy, that was a tough day," he puffed.

2 "Now, where's my left ear? And my hat?" He began to collect his parts from all around the playroom and put himself back together again.

3 "Nearly done. Just my nose to find!" Mr Potato Head said, happily. He searched and searched, but his nose was nowhere to be found.

4 The other toys couldn't sniff out the missing nose either. "Don't worry, my darling. I'm sure it'll turn up soon," Mrs Potato Head told him.

5 In the meantime, the toys decided to find a new nose for Mr Potato Head. "I'm not sure about this jigsaw piece," he told Buzz.

6 "Well, what about using one of my coins instead?" Hamm suggested. "Maybe ... But it's just not the same," sighed Mr Potato Head.

Colour in Lotso!

7 "Guys, I give up. I miss my real nose!" Mr Potato Head wailed. The toys didn't like seeing their friend upset but they had run out of ideas.

8 "Hang on!" Lotso cried, suddenly. "Where would you go if you were a nose? Somewhere that smells good, of course! Follow me!"

11

MMMM!

9 Lotso led them across the playroom. Sure enough, snuggled up on Lotso's strawberry-scented truck was Mr Potato Head's nose!

10 "Naughty nose, there you are!" Mr Potato Head cried, happy again. "And next time you go missing, I'll know exactly where to look!"

THE END

About the story

1 What part of Mr Potato Head went missing?

....

2 What did Buzz stick onto Mr Potato Head's face?

....

3 Who suggested a coin?

....

Answers on page 68.

Colouring Cowboys

Help Woody finish and colour in the picture.

Woody is having fun drawing Bullseye. What do you think of his artwork?

13

Prickly Puzzles

Mr Pricklepants has some puzzles to solve. Can you help him?

Shadow play

Tick the box next to the shadow that belongs to Mr Pricklepants.

Odd one out

Can you help Mr Pricklepants spot the odd one out in the row of Hamm piggy banks?

1 2 3 4

Dotty time

Who is the mysterious toy hiding in the picture below? Join the dots to find out.

Movie fact
Mr Pricklepants' unicorn friend is called Buttercup.

Answers on page 68.

15

Toy Tumble

The toys are all jumbled up in their toy box. Can you spot six differences in the picture opposite?

Point to Hamm.

How many balls can you count on these pages?

Can you spot Buzz?

Colour a star as you spot each difference

Answers on page 68.

Draw your favourite toy in this space.

Make Bullseye's Buddy

Make a brilliant horse puppet out of an old sock!

You will need

- An old sock
- Newspaper
- Elastic
- Four cotton reels
- Coloured felt
- Safety scissors
- Glue

1 Stuff some scrunched-up pieces of newspaper into a knee-length sock.

2 Cut out two eyes, two ears, a mane and a saddle from felt.

3 Cut two lengths of elastic. Thread a cotton reel on to each end and tie a knot in the elastic to hold them in place.

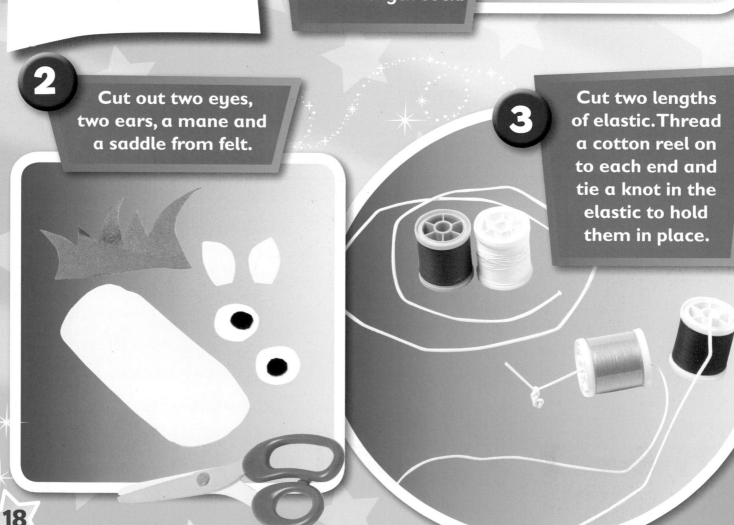

4 Cut two more lengths of elastic and tie one onto each end of the sock.

Ask an adult to help.

5 Hang the elastic with the cotton reels over the top of the sock. Glue on the eyes, ears, mane and saddle and your puppet is ready to play!

Use the long pieces of elastic to make your horse trot!

Hide-and-Seek

1 One day, Woody and the rest of the toys were in the mood for some fun! "Let's play hide-and-seek," suggested Woody.

2 "The last toy to be found will be the winner," explained Woody. He began to count to 20 and the other toys dashed off to hide.

OOOH!

3 "We must find a great hiding place, because Woody is really good at seeking!" Rex told Trixie. "No problem!" Trixie replied.

4 The other toys quickly hid too, but the aliens didn't know where to go. "Oooh!" they cried, as they scurried around in a panic.

5 A little while later, Woody had found everyone apart from one of the aliens. Woody noticed the three peas and it gave him an idea.

6 Woody unzipped the peas' pod. Sure enough, the alien was snoozing inside! "Meee win?" he asked, as he woke up with a yawn.

THE END

About the story

a What game were the toys playing?

....

b Who counted to 20?

....

c Who didn't know where to hide?

....

Answers on page 68.

Ride Home

Help Jessie, Woody and Bullseye avoid Chunk and choose the right path to Andy's house on Elm Street.

1 **2** **3**

SUNNYSIDE
DAYCARE

Count the sheriff badges.

Elm Street

Answers on page 68.

Who is it?

Oh no! There's a toy left in the box for Sunnyside. Can you guess from the clues below who it is?

He is green.

He has sharp teeth.

He has a tail.

Toy Search

Cross off all the letters that appear more than once in the grid below to find out the name of a toy friend.

P	S	P	L	I	T
B	N	K	T	Y	B
M	D	M	O	G	P

To Infinity!

Race to help Buzz blast off to infinity and beyond!

START

1 2 3
9 10 11 12 13
14 15 16 17
23 24 25 26 27
28 29 30

24

Take it in turns to throw the dice and move around the board. If you land on a picture, follow the instruction in the key. The first one to the finish is the winner.

To infinity and beyond!

You will need
- A dice
- Two counters

KEY

Shoot ahead! Move forward 2 spaces.

Zoom off! Move forward 4 spaces.

Burn out! Miss a go.

In a spin! Go back 3 spaces.

DISNEY·PIXAR MONSTERS, INC.

Meet the Scream Team

In the city of Monstropolis lives a gang of the scariest monsters, and they all work at Monsters, Inc.

SULLEY
He's the top monster with a scare record to die for! Mike is Sulley's best monster mate.

BOO
A little girl with pigtails and a giggle, Boo is two and not afraid of monsters – or anything else!

MIKE

Like a giant pea with a single eye, Mike is round and green, with a cheeky grin. He tells jokes and has a soft spot for Celia.

Movie fact
At first, Mike is scared of Boo but he soon realises she's harmless!

CELIA

She's sweet, with snaky hair and slinky legs, and she works as company receptionist.

MR WATERNOOSE

Big boss of the company and crabby with it, Mr Waternoose gives the orders.

RANDALL

Watch out for sneaky Randall. He creeps around and changes colour to match his surroundings.

a   b   c

Here are three scream canisters. Can you spot the odd one out?

Answer on page 68.

The Scarebot

Waternoose has hired a new robot, but will it be scarier than Sulley?

1 One morning, on the Scare Floor at Monsters, Inc., Waternoose made an announcement. "You've been working far too hard lately, Sulley," he said.

2 "I have?" Sulley replied. He was confused. Waternoose nodded and showed Sulley a new robot. "This is the Scarebot 5000," he explained.

3 "The Scarebot can scare up screams as well as the top Scarers," Waternoose told Sulley. "It will make your job easier!"

4 "The Scarebot will be a big help!" Mike laughed. "Now you can take a break anytime you like!" he told Sulley.

5 But Sulley wasn't impressed. "I don't need a robot's help," he muttered, as he marched past the Scarebot and through a door to collect a new scream.

6 Mike insisted that the Scarebot help. Sulley was getting bored, sitting around and waiting for the Scarebot to finish his scaring.

7 "I'm tired of waiting for a robot to do my job!" Sulley groaned, later. "Now it's your turn," Mike shouted. "The Scarebot's been in that room too long!"

8 Inside the room, Sulley found the Scarebot. But it wasn't scaring anyone! It had found a happy boy, who loved robots!

9 As the Scarebot and the boy played, Sulley made his scariest face. The boy jumped off the Scarebot and ran back to his bed, screaming.

10 On the Scare Floor, Sulley explained that the Scarebot wasn't scary enough. "You can out-scare any robot, Sulley!" Waternoose chuckled.

THE END

About the story

a What was the robot called?

....

b Who said the robot would be a big help?

....

c What did the boy love?

....

d Who made their scariest face?

....

30

Answers on page 68.

Who's There?

Draw a picture of the monster you think is hiding behind Boo's door.

Funny Faces

Mike makes funny faces! Match the pictures to the words below, then trace over the letters.

1

2

3

a sad

b angry

c happy

Movie fact
Celia calls Mike her 'Googly Bear'!

Answers on page 68.

Can you spot the shadow that matches Celia exactly? Draw a circle around it.

1 2 3 4

Answer on page 68.

Add some colour to this picture of sneaky Randall.

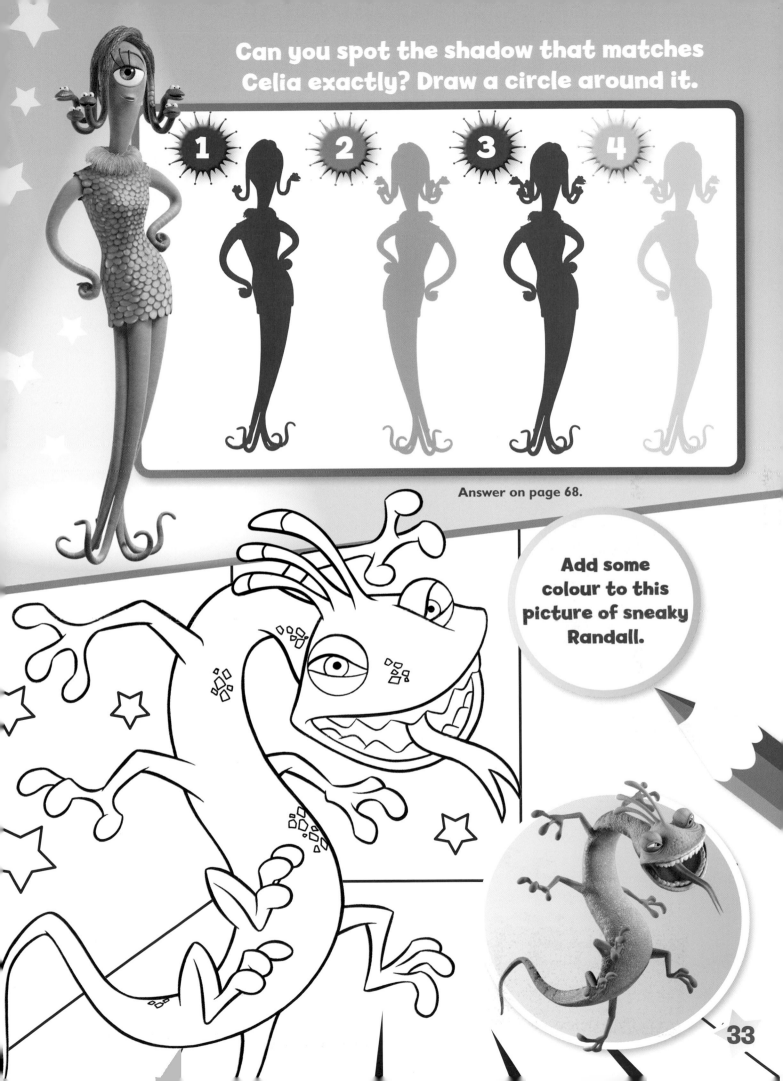

33

Draw Mike

Use these steps as a guide to draw a brilliant picture of Mike.

1

2

3

4

Use a pencil at first, then go over the lines you want to keep in pen. Finally, add some colour to Mike!

34

Roar Score

Sulley is an expert at roaring!

Use the code below to work out how many screams Sulley has collected behind each door.

 = 1   = 2   = 3

a

b

Write your answer here.

Answers on page 69.

Write your answer here.

Monster Pad

Make drawing monstrously fun with this great pad of paper!

You will need

- A pad of paper
- Green felt
- An empty yogurt pot or container
- Black and green paint
- A ping-pong ball
- Green card
- Scissors and glue

1 Cut the felt to fit the front of the pad and stick it to the cover.

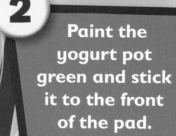

2 Paint the yogurt pot green and stick it to the front of the pad.

3 Ask an adult to help you cut the ping-pong ball in half. Then paint on an eyeball.

4 Cut the green card into eight thin strips. Take two strips and fold them over each other. Repeat to make two arms and two legs.

5 Glue the ping-pong ball and strips of card to the yogurt tub to make Mike's eye, arms and legs.

Ask an adult to help.

37

The Big Scare

Randall is willing to take a risk to become number one on the Monsters, Inc. scare board. But will his risk pay off?

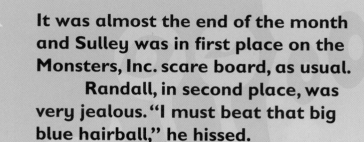

It was almost the end of the month and Sulley was in first place on the Monsters, Inc. scare board, as usual.

Randall, in second place, was very jealous. "I must beat that big blue hairball," he hissed.

So, Randall sneaked into the part of the building where the doors were stored. He discovered some doors that were being kept separately. Each door had a sticker that said **WARNING! EXPERIMENTAL DOOR.**

"I'll beat Sulley!" Randall sniggered, sending one of the doors to his scare station.

When Randall stepped through, he found himself in a room full of children at a summer camp. When they saw Randall, they screamed loud enough to fill ten whole canisters!

Mike gulped when he saw that Randall had a big lead on the scare board. "I need to get my top spot back," said Sulley.

It was hard work but Sulley just managed to regain the lead. Randall was furious.

"I want the loudest scream Monsters, Inc. has ever heard!"

TOP SCARER

TOP SCARER

he cried, running back towards the experimental doors.

"There must be lots of little ones behind this," he sniggered, sending a big metal door to his scare station.

It was very dark inside but Randall could see a group cuddled together. "RAAA!" yelled Randall, expecting to hear children scream.

But instead of children, lion cubs began to whimper! Randall was in a cage at a zoo! Randall scrambled back to the scare floor, as an angry adult lion pounced. Randall screamed louder than anyone at Monsters, Inc. had ever heard!

"Randall, your scream doesn't count," giggled Mike.

Mike pointed to the scare board. Sulley was in first place!

Mike and Sulley cheered as Randall sloped off with his tail between his legs!

THE END

Movie fact
Sneaky Randall can change colour to blend into the background.

39

Mike's Jokes

Mike loves making his friends giggle.

Laugh along with these great jokes.

How do you get a baby astronaut to sleep? You rock-it!

Ha ha!

What's purple and green with red spots? Sulley with the measles!

How do fish get to school? By octobus!

Hee hee!

When do astronauts eat? At launch time!

Why did the whale cross the road? To get to the other tide!

Messing it Up

Sulley and Boo have made a monster-sized mess! Finish the picture with your messiest colours.

Can you spot this object in the scene? Tick the box when you spot it.

Knock! Knock! Beware!

You will need
- coloured pens
- a dice

Mike and Sulley are racing to collect the most screams from the scare doors.

1

2

3

4

5

6

How to play

Decide to be Mike or Sulley. Take it in turns to throw the dice. Colour in the scare door that matches the number thrown. Miss a go if you have already coloured in the door. Door 1 is Boo's door, so miss a go if you throw a 1. The first player to colour in all their doors has collected the most screams and is the winner.

1

2

3

5

4

6

Monster Time

How well do you know the world of Monsters, Inc.?
Here's your chance to find out.

1 What is the name of the city where all the monsters live?

a Mongolia
b Monstropolis
c London

2 Who is the top scarer at Monsters, Inc.?

a Sulley
b Mike
c Randall

3 Who is Sulley's best friend?

a Celia
b Waternoose
c Mike

4 Which monster has snakes for hair?

a Mike
b Celia
c Roz

5 How does Randall melt into the background?

a He burps loudly
b He changes colour
c He goes to sleep

6 Who likes making his monster mates laugh?

a Sulley
b Randall
c Mike

Answers on page 69.

Fishy Tales

What do you find in Finding Nemo? Lots of fun characters and an exciting adventure, that's what!

Barrier Reef beginnings

Marlin lives in the reef with his son **Nemo**. Disaster strikes when **Nemo** is caught by a scuba diver. **Marlin** sets out to find him, helped by **Dory**. They ask around. Can **Bruce** and his shark friends help?

A clue!

While straight-talking with the **sharks**, **Marlin** finds the scuba diver's mask. The address on it reads: Sydney, Australia! Where's that? **Marlin** and **Dory** must find out!

Just keep swimmin'!

In the East Australian Current, a surfing turtle called **Crush** takes **Dory** and **Marlin** for a ride. **Crush** has plenty of turtle friends and the story of **Marlin's** search spreads to Sydney.

Dental trouble

In Sydney harbour, a dentist has dropped poor **Nemo** into a fish tank in his office. He plans to give **Nemo** to his nasty niece. But **Marlin** is not far away!

To the rescue!

There's high drama as **Nemo** escapes through a drain. **Marlin** arrives in a whale's mouth. After a long, dangerous journey, father and son are reunited. They swim back to the warm waters of home.

These two turtles are not the same. Can you spot four differences in the picture on the right?

Answer on page 69.

Marlin's Trick

1 One day, Marlin and Nemo were playing on the coral reef when a barracuda with razor-sharp teeth swam by. "Here comes trouble!" said Marlin.

2 All the fish disappeared into the sea. "I thought we were safe on the coral reef!" groaned Nemo, as he followed Marlin into some seaweed.

3 Nemo and Marlin peeked out from the seaweed. They could see the barracuda chasing fish around the reef. "We can't hide forever," said Marlin.

4 Marlin and Nemo rushed towards a sea anemone, but the barracuda spotted them and stayed close. "I'm scared!" said Nemo.

5 "The anemone's stings will keep us safe," said Marlin. That gave him an idea. "Wait here!" he told Nemo. "I'll teach that barracuda a lesson!"

6 Marlin swam out and stopped right in front of the barracuda, "Bet you can't catch me, you bully!" he cried, as he raced off into the ocean.

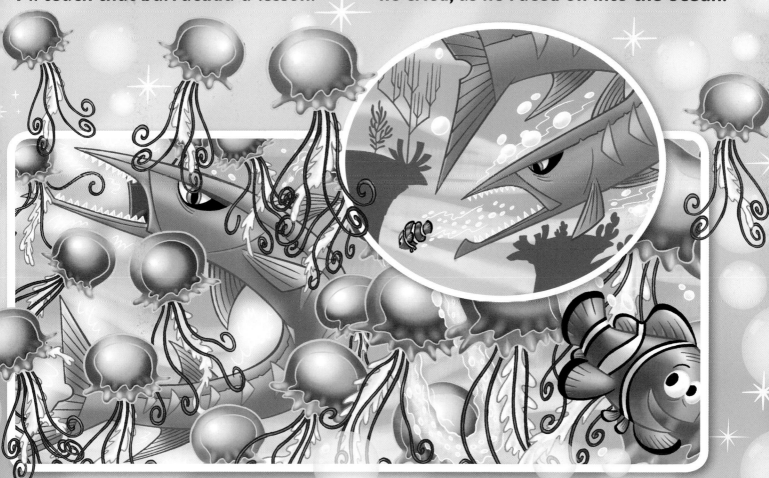

7 The barracuda followed Marlin ... right into a group of jellyfish. "Ouch! Ouch!" cried the barracuda as the jellyfish stung him all over!

8 Marlin swam back to the reef. "Everyone can come out now, it's safe!" he called. All the fish flapped their fins and cheered.

THE END

How to Draw Nemo

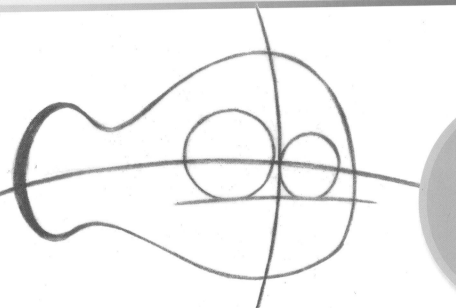

50

3

Rub out the guidelines. Draw stripes onto the body and fins.

4

Go over the lines in black pen or pencil and colour in the pupils. Finish your drawing of Nemo by adding some colour!

Movie fact
Nemo is a clownfish. Clownfish are stripy and small, and like to live in warm waters.

Turtle Time

Marlin and Dory are racing along with the sea turtles.
How fast can you find the answers to these questions?

1 How many turtles can you count?

Yippeee!

Wheeeeee!

2 Who is swimming upside down?

....

3 Who is getting a lift from Crush?

....

Yahaah!

4 How many turtles have their eyes closed?

Wahooo!

Movie fact
Every summer, Crush and his pals surf on the East Australian Current, all the way to Sydney Harbour.

Answers on page 69.

53

Who Said What?

How well do you know the characters from Finding Nemo?

Match the words to the right speech bubble.

Write the correct number or words in the speech bubble next to each character. Use the close-ups to help.

1 "Just keep swimming."

2 "Where's my son?"

3 "See this tentacle?"

4 "The name's Crush."

5 "I wanna go home."

6 "I'm H2O intolerant."

WALL·E's World

How well do you know WALL·E's world? Answer true or false to each of these statements.

WALL·E

1 WALL·E crushes the rubbish he finds into a cube.

TRUE   FALSE

2 WALL·E finds a plant amongs the rubbish.

TRUE   FALSE

3 WALL·E's pet is a spider.

TRUE   FALSE

Follow the line with your finger.

Movie fact
WALL·E collects human objects that he finds amongst the rubbish.

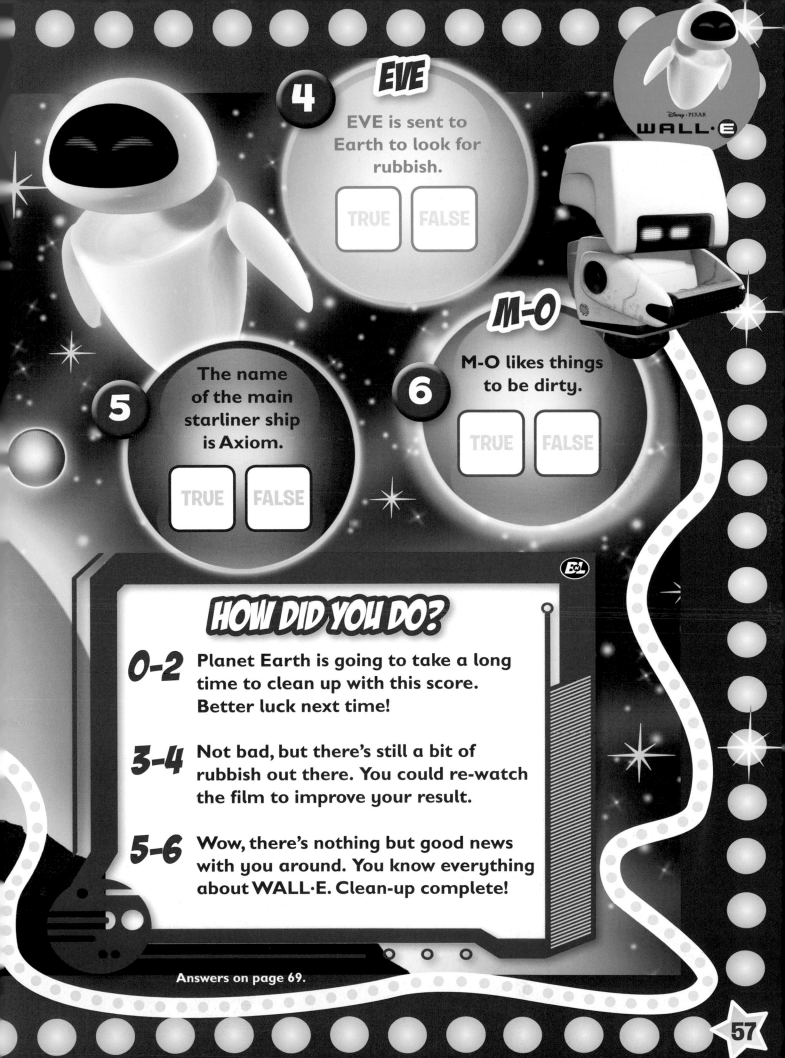

EVE

4 EVE is sent to Earth to look for rubbish.

TRUE   FALSE

5 The name of the main starliner ship is Axiom.

TRUE   FALSE

M-O

6 M-O likes things to be dirty.

TRUE   FALSE

HOW DID YOU DO?

0-2 Planet Earth is going to take a long time to clean up with this score. Better luck next time!

3-4 Not bad, but there's still a bit of rubbish out there. You could re-watch the film to improve your result.

5-6 Wow, there's nothing but good news with you around. You know everything about WALL·E. Clean-up complete!

Answers on page 69.

WALL·E

Disney · PIXAR

Bubble Trouble

WALL·E finds something soapy in the trash,
but it's the cockroach who's in for a surprise!

1 WALL·E was trawling through rubbish to find things to make into a trash tower. His pet cockroach scurried about while he worked.

2 Just then, WALL·E found a new treasure! It was a bottle of liquid soap. WALL·E inspected it. It was smooth and shiny and gloopy.

3 When WALL·E gave the bottle a little squeeze, lots of pretty soapy bubbles came out. "Oooh!" beeped WALL·E, excitedly.

4 WALL·E and the bubbles danced around. "Heee!" WALL·E laughed as some of the bubbles popped on his metal surface and tickled him.

5 Suddenly, the cockroach began to float away! He'd been watching WALL·E when he got trapped inside a bubble. "Eeeeek!" WALL·E cried.

6 WALL·E wanted to rescue his friend. He found a long flagpole and grabbed it with his claws. WALL·E used it to pop the bubble.

7 With the bubble gone, the poor cockroach began to fall. WALL·E panicked. He picked up the bottle and caught his falling friend just in time.

8 WALL·E began to dance again, keeping his friend safe in his hands. Lots and lots of soapy bubbles poured out of the bottle!

THE END

Control Panel

How quickly can you help WALL·E complete these fun activities

1 How many levers can you count?

2 Point to planet Earth.

3 Colour the box the same colour as the button WALL·E is about to press.

60

Answers on page 69.

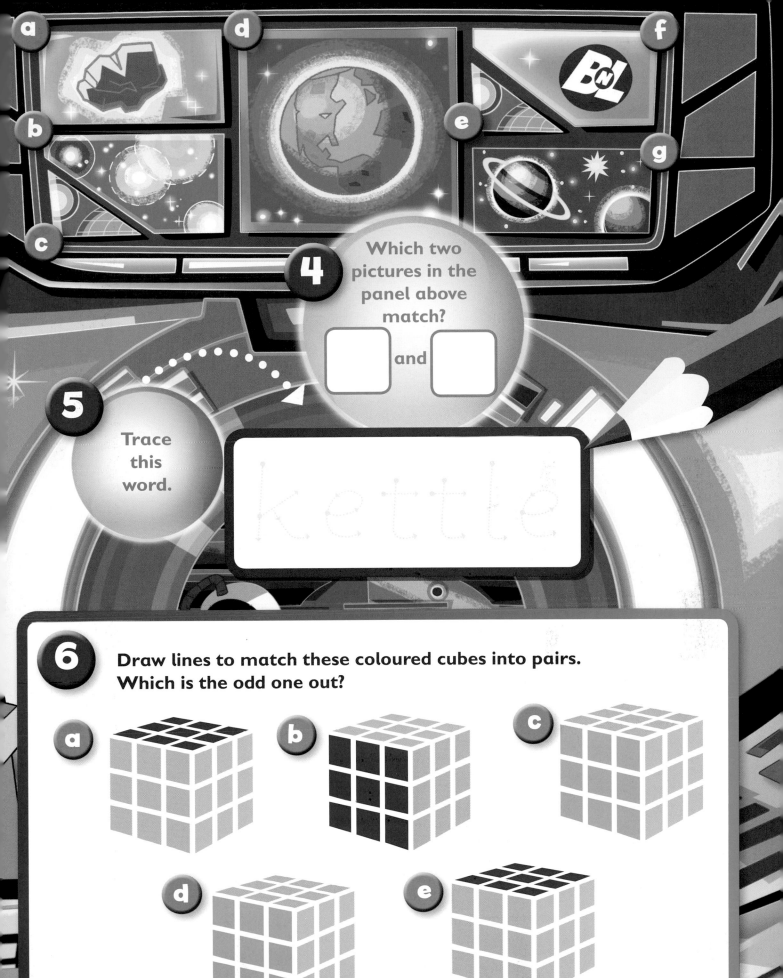

a **d** **f**

e

b

g

c

4 Which two pictures in the panel above match?

☐ and ☐

5 Trace this word.

kettle

6 Draw lines to match these coloured cubes into pairs. Which is the odd one out?

a **b** **c**

d **e**

Meet the Family

This is one very talented family! Can you match each of the Supers to their description?

Write the correct number in the star beside each character.

1 She's super-flexible and very streeeeetchy!

2 This superhero has the power of super strength!

3 This is one speedy ten-year-old!

4 She's a shy teenager who can turn invisible!

5 This two-year-old hasn't found his power yet!

ELASTIGIRL

Undercover name: Helen Parr

JACK-JACK

Undercover name: Jack-Jack Parr

VIOLET

Undercover name: Violet Parr

MR INCREDIBLE

Undercover name: Bob Parr

DASH

Undercover name: Dashiel Parr

THE BADDIE!

Villain Syndrome is the arch-enemy of Mr Incredible and his family. With no super powers of his own, Syndrome created a gigantic robot that only he can control.

Island Rescue

Elastigirl, Dash and Violet are heading to Nomanisan Island to rescue Mr Incredible. Answer these questions about the scene.

1 What has Elastigirl stretched into?

_ _ _ _ _ _ _ _

2 Who is powering the boat with his super-fast running?

_ _ _ _ _ _ _ _

3 Can you spot the villain, Syndrome?

Movie fact
Although Dash has lots of high-speed crashes, he never ever gets hurt!

64

Answers on page 69.

4 How many Velocipods can you count?

5 Can you find a rock that looks like one of the Incredibles?

Movie fact
Elastigirl is great at hiding – she can make herself as thin as 1mm!

6 Which detail below is not from the main picture?

Movie fact
When he was young, Syndrome wanted to be Mr Incredible's smart sidekick.

a **b** **c** **d** **e**

65

Crack the Code

Dash and Violet are using a secret code to tell you what they think of you! Can you use the key below to crack it?

d= ■
m= ★
t= ✴
r= ➤
s= ●
a= S
k= ▲
i= O

Write your answer in the boxes below.

Answers on page 69.

66

Answers

Pages 8-9

Toy Friend? Toy Foe?

Friends
Woody
Jessie
Mr Potato Head
Buzz Lightyear
Aliens

Foes
Big Baby
Lotso

Page 12

About the story

1. Nose
2. Jigsaw piece
3. Hamm

Pages 14-15

Prickly Puzzles

Shadow 4 belongs to Mr Pricklepants.

Hamm 2 is the odd one out.

An alien is hiding in the picture.

Page 17

Toy Tumble

There are 4 balls.

Pages 20-21

About the story

a. Hide-and-seek
b. Woody
c. The aliens

Pages 22-23

Ride Home

Path 1 leads to Elm Street.

There are 7 sheriff badges.

Who is it?

Rex is in the box.

Toy Search

Slinky Dog

Pages 26-27

Meet the Scream Team

b is the odd one out.

Page 30

About the story

a. Scarebot 5000
b. Mike
c. Robots
d. Sulley

Pages 32-33

Funny Faces

1. c - happy
2. b - angry
3. a - sad

Shadow 3 matches Celia.

Pages 35

Roar Score

Door a - 17 screams
Door b - 11 screams

Pages 44-45

Monster Time

1. b   4. b
2. a   5. b
3. c   6. c

Page 47

Fishy Tales

Pages 52-53

Turtle Time   3. Marlin
1. 11   4. 2
2. Dory

Pages 54-55

Who Said What?

1. Dory   4. Crush
2. Marlin 5. Nemo
3. Pearl   6. Sheldon

Pages 56-57

WALL·E's World

1. True   4. False
2. True   5. True
3. False   6. False

Pages 60-61

Control Panel

1. 1   4. c and e
3. Red   6. a and e, c and d.
            Cube b is the odd one out.

Pages 62-63

Meet the Family

1. Elastigirl   4. Violet
2. Mr Incredible   5. Jack-Jack
3. Dash

Pages 64-65

Island Rescue

1. A boat   4. 5
2. Dash   6. b
3. On the rocks

Page 66

Crack the Code

Smart kid